P9-CLR-372

Little Bear says:
"When you see a fragrance label,
scratch it with your fingernail.
You will smell Christmas, too."

The Sweet Smell of Christmas

By Patricia Scarry • Illustrated by J. P. Miller

A GOLDEN BOOK • NEW YORK

Copyright © 1970, renewed 1998 by Random House, Inc. All rights reserved under International and Pan-American Copyright Conventions. Published in the United States by Golden Books, an imprint of Random House Children's Books, a division of Random House, Inc., New York, and simultaneously in Canada by Random House of Canada Limited, Toronto. Golden Books, A Golden Book, A Golden Scratch and Sniff Book, and the G colophon are registered trademarks of Random House, Inc. Originally published in 1970 by Golden Books Publishing Company, Inc. First Random House Edition 2003. Library of Congress Control Number: 2002116836
ISBN: 0-375-82643-2 www.goldenbooks.com
Manufactured in the United States of America 10 9 8 7 6 5 4 3

One morning, Little Bear sat up in bed and sniffed and sniffed with his nose. ''Something wonderful is going to happen,'' he said. ''My nose tells me so.''

Little Bear ran downstairs to the kitchen. "Mommy, what do I smell?" he asked. "Christmas is coming. I think that's what you smell," said Mother Bear. "When will Christmas be here, mommy?"

"Christmas will be here tomorrow. I'm baking this apple pie for Christmas." Little Bear sniffed at the pie. It smelled delicious! "Yes, I can smell Christmas. It's coming soon," he said.

Here is Bear's apple pie.
Can you smell Christmas, too?

After breakfast, Father Bear pulled Little Bear on his sled. "Are we going to find Christmas, daddy?" asked Bear.
"No, we are going to find a nice little pine tree to take home for our Christmas tree," said father.

They searched in the woods until they found a bushy little pine tree. Father chopped it down with his axe and put it on the sled.

Little Bear helped pull the tree home over the snow. It was a nice fresh tree, and it smelled so piney. Little Bear poked his nose into the branches and sniffed a deep sniff. "Now I can smell Christmas," he said. "It's not far away."

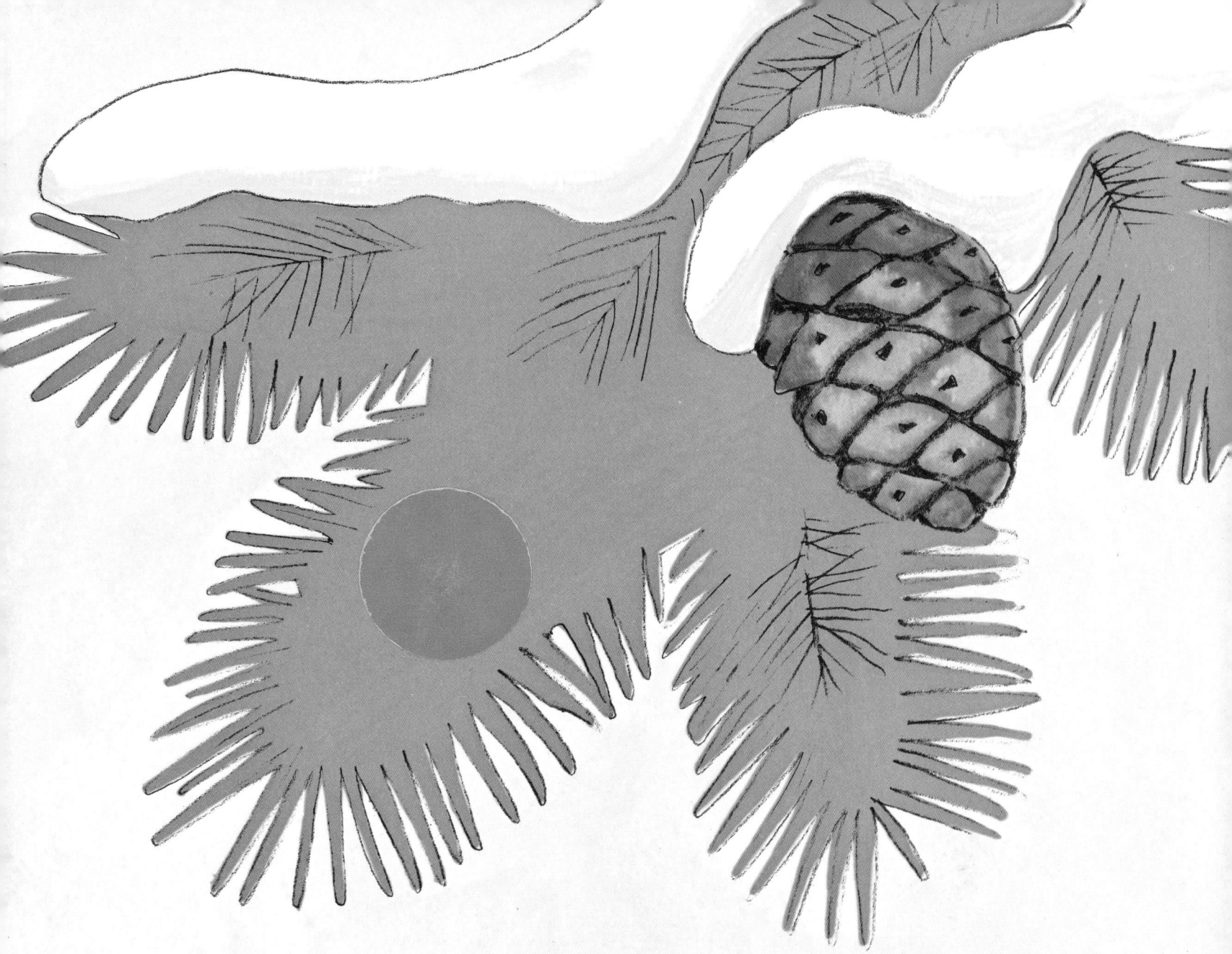

You smell the pine tree, too.
Doesn't it smell nice?

Then the Bear family trimmed their tree. It was fun! They hung lovely glass balls and silvery tinsel on the branches. On the very top, father put a beautiful star.

"Something is missing," said mother. "What can it be?"

She hurried to the kitchen. When she came back, she was carrying a big jar. "Candy canes," she said. "We forgot to put candy canes on our tree."

Bear held a candy cane in his paw and sniffed. "Mmmm, I can smell Christmas. It's coming very soon!" he said.

Here is a candy cane
for you to sniff.

Can you smell
Christmas coming?

Little Bear hung the candy canes on the branches. At last, the tree was finished. And, oh my, it was so beautiful! Little Bear jumped up and down and clapped his paws.

Mother Bear was working in the kitchen.
"What are you making, mommy?"
asked Bear.
"Gingerbread boys," said mother.
"You may help me."
Bear liked doing that. He cut out the gingerbread boys with a little tin cutter.
Then he made their funny faces.
And when he smelled them cooking,
Bear said, "Mmmm, I can smell
Christmas. It's almost here!"

This is your gingerbread boy.
Does it smell like Christmas, too?

While Bear was hanging a gingerbread boy on the tree, he heard singing at the window. There, in the snow, were some carolers. How lovely it was to hear Christmas music in the frosty night.

Mother Bear invited the carolers indoors for some steaming hot chocolate. Bear had some, too. He put his nose down close to his cup. The hot chocolate smelled sweet and chocolatey. "Oh, now I can smell Christmas," Bear said. "It's going to happen right away!"

Now you smell the hot chocolate.
Mmmm. It smells so good.

Bear was right. It was almost Christmas. The Bear family hung their stockings by the fireplace. Then Little Bear hurried to bed. He listened for Santa's reindeer landing on the roof. He listened and listened. Then he fell asleep.

"Ho! Ho! Ho!" laughed merry Santa Claus, as he slid down the chimney. "My, what a pretty tree," he said, nibbling a gingerbread boy, "and what a good little bear lives here. I will leave him lots of toys." He dug in his toysack and put everything a bear could dream of under the tree.

At last, it was morning. Little Bear woke up.
He sniffed. He said, "It's Christmas day at last!"
Then he ran downstairs to find his stocking. There
was a big juicy orange on top, and down inside,
Bear found a little red train, a storybook,
a tiny ball, and candies and puzzles.
Bear sniffed at his orange.
"Now I know it's Christmas!" he said.
And he ate that orange up.

Here is a
Christmas orange
for you.

Can you smell Christmas now?

Mother and Father Bear hurried downstairs to open their presents, too. There was a nice tie for father, and warm mittens. Mother found a necklace and lots of pretty things.
And under the tree for Little Bear were a big red scooter, a drum, a little toy horse, a bugle and a big striped ball. Best of all, there was a soft furry teddy bear, a Christmas friend for Bear. All the Bears agreed it was the happiest Christmas ever!